For my dad,
who showed me that real men are sensitive, kind,
and feel their feelings with pride.

IMPRINT
A part of Macmillan Publishing Group, LLC
175 Fifth Avenue, New York, NY 10010

ABOUT THIS BOOK
The art in this book was created digitally. The text was set in Filson Soft.
This book was edited by Erin Stein and designed by Natalie C. Sousa.
The production was supervised by Raymond Ernesto Colón, and the production editor was Dawn Ryan.

Harrison Dwight, Ballerina and Knight. Text copyright © 2019 by Ray Mac Productions, Inc.
All rights reserved. Printed in the United States of America by Worzalla, Stevens Point, Wisconsin.

Our books may be purchased in bulk for promotional, educational, or business use. Please contact your local bookseller
or the Macmillan Corporate and Premium Sales Department at (800) 221-7945 ext. 5442
or by email at MacmillanSpecialMarkets@macmillan.com.

Library of Congress Cataloging-in-Publication Data is available.
ISBN 978-1-250-13858-3

Imprint logo designed by Amanda Spielman

First edition, 2019

1 3 5 7 9 10 8 6 4 2

mackids.com

Calling all knights! Please stand guard for this book!
Save it from knaves or an evil book crook!
Calling ballerinas! Don't let thieves this book take,
or they'll find themselves lost in the depths of Swan Lake!

Harrison Dwight
Ballerina and Knight

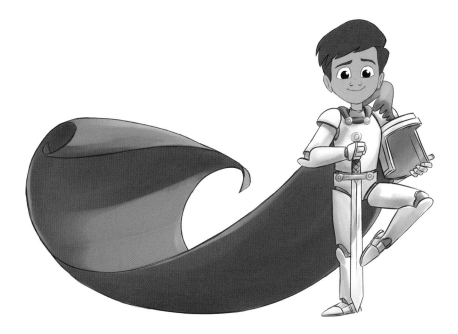

written by **Rachael MacFarlane**   illustrated by **Spencer Laudiero**

{Imprint} MAKE YOUR MARK

New York

My name is Harrison—
Harrison Dwight.

I'm a ballet dancer.
I'm also a knight!

When I spin and I leap, it makes me feel strong,
like the world is my stage and it dances along!

My armor is silver and shiny and bright.

It protects me from things that go bump in the night.

When I fall on the playground, it hurts, so I cry.

I don't hold back my tears. I don't even try.

My dad says to feel all my feelings with pride.

Don't pretend they're not there, or hide them inside.

Sometimes my friends and I just don't agree.
Should we go storm a castle or climb a tall tree?

Fighting is no way to solve what's gone wrong.

If we just talk it out, we can all get along.

I watch football with Mom and we cheer on our team,

then pick flowers with Dad by our favorite stream.

I love painting my toes in orange or pink!

Who says pink is for girls? Pink is just pink!

It takes lots of courage
to feel what you feel.

It helps you move past it and helps you to heal.

I heard someone once say that boys shouldn't cry.

But boys feel things too. It's okay, and here's why . . .

We all have big feelings we carry inside,

like love, fear, and sadness. Our hearts open wide!

These feelings inside are what make you, YOU!

Letting them out helps the world know you, too.

The best you can be is just who you are,

whether crossing home plate or at the ballet barre.

I am both a dancer
and a brave and bold knight.

But more than all that, I'm just Harrison Dwight!